The Pig in the Pond

Martin Waddell

illustrated by Jill Barton

CANDLEWICK PRESS
CAMBRIDGE, MASSACHUSETTS

For Charlotte Maeve
M.W.

For Porky Boffin
J.B.

First U.S. edition 1992
First published in Great Britain in 1992 by Walker Books Ltd., London.

ISBN 1-56402-050-9
Library of Congress Catalog Card Number 91-58751
Library of Congress Cataloging-in-Publication information is available.

10 9 8 7 6 5 4 3 2 1

Printed and bound in Hong Kong

The pictures in this book were done in watercolor and pencil.

Candlewick Press
2067 Massachusetts Avenue
Cambridge, Massachusetts 02140

This is the story of Neligan's pig.

One day Neligan went into town.

It was hot. It was dry.

The sun shone in the sky.

Neligan's pig sat by

Neligan's pond.

The ducks went, "Quack!"
The geese went, "Honk!"
They were cool on
the water in
Neligan's pond.

The pig sat in the sun.

She looked at the pond.

The ducks went, "Quack!"

The geese went, "Honk!"

The pig went, "Oink!"

She didn't go in,

because pigs don't swim.

The pig sat in the sun getting hotter and hotter.

The ducks went, "Quack, quack!"   The geese went, "Honk, honk!"

The pig went, "Oink, oink!" She didn't go in, because pigs don't swim.

The pig gulped and gasped and looked at the water.

The ducks went, "Quack, quack, quack!"

The geese went, "Honk, honk, honk!"

The pig went, "Oink, oink, oink!"

She rose from the ground

and turned around

and around,

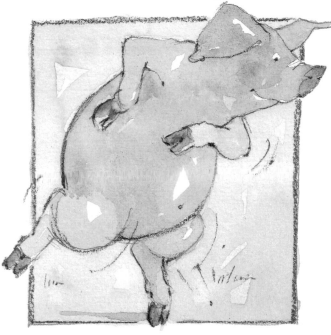

stamping her feet

and twirling her tail,

and . . .

SPLASH!

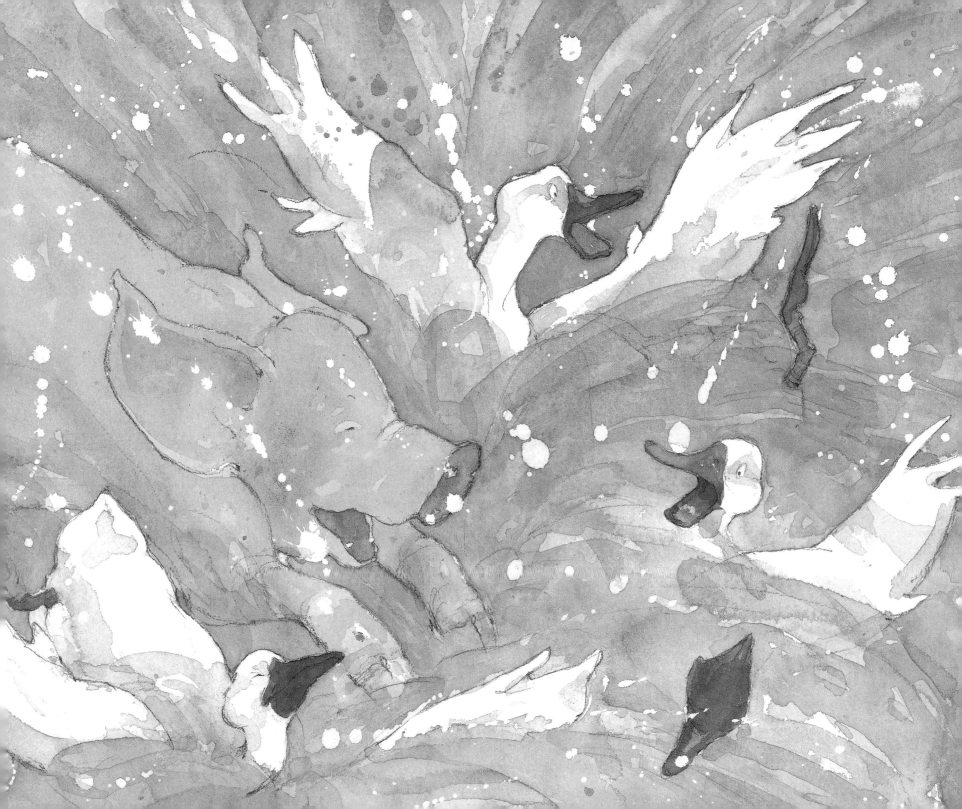

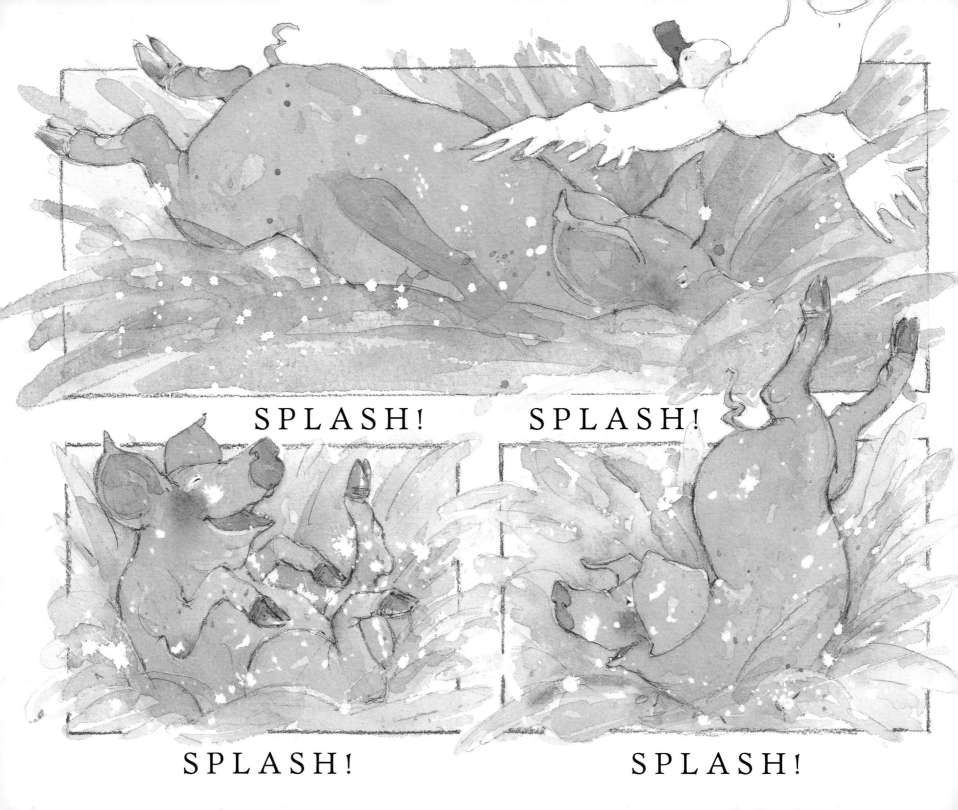

SPLASH!   SPLASH!

SPLASH!   SPLASH!

SPLASH! SPLASH!

SPLASH! SPLASH!

The ducks and the geese were splashed out of the pond.

The ducks went, "Quack, quack, quack, quack!"
The geese went, "Honk, honk, honk, honk!"
which means, very loudly, "The pig's in the pond!"

"The pig's in the pond!"

"The pig's in the pond!"

The word spread about, above, and beyond,

"The pig's in the pond!" "The pig's in the pond!"

"At Neligan's farm, the pig's in the pond!"

From the fields all around they came to see
the pig in the pond at Neligan's farm.
And then . . .

Neligan came on his cart!

Neligan looked at the pig in the pond.

The pig went, "Oink!"

Neligan took off his hat.

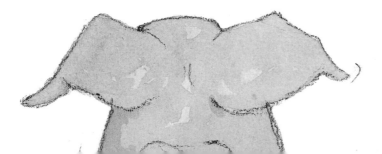

Neligan looked at the pig in the pond.

The pig went, "Oink, oink!"

Neligan took off his pants and boots.

Neligan looked at the pig in the pond.

The pig went, "Oink, oink, oink!"

Neligan took off his shirt.

Neligan looked at the pig in the pond.

The pig went, "Oink, oink, oink, OINK!"

Neligan took off his underwear and . . .

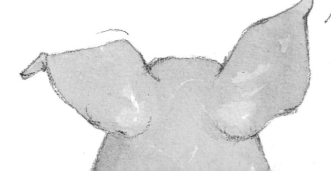

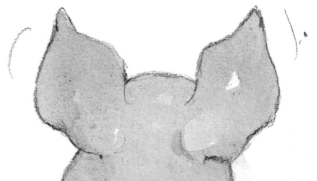

SPLASH! Neligan joined the pig in the pond.

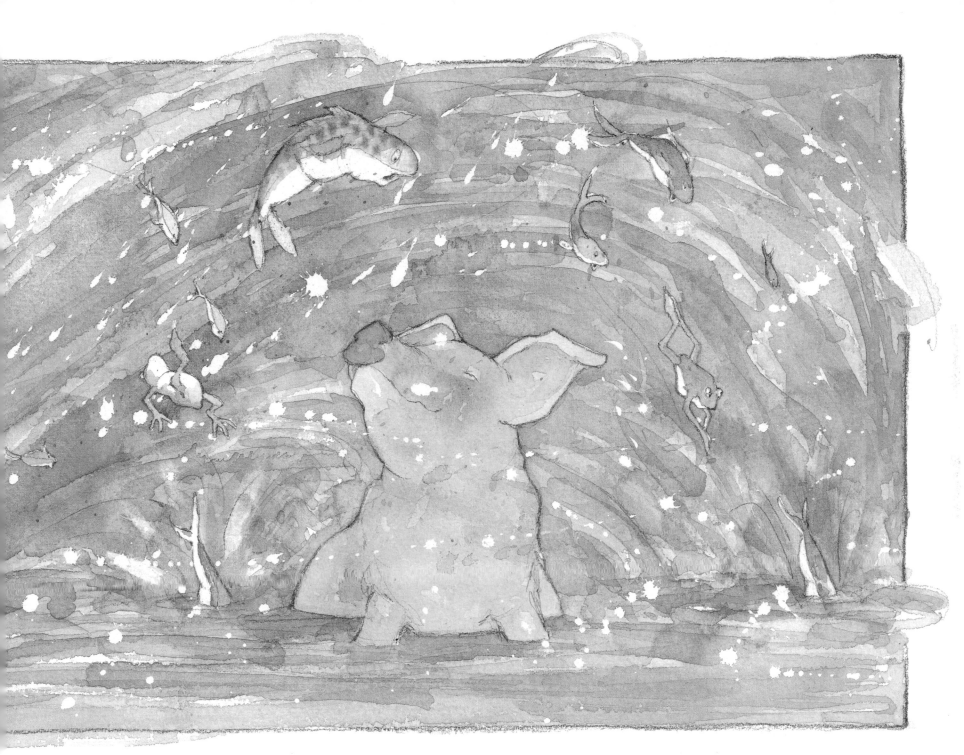

What happened next?

SPLO

OOOOOOSH!

They all joined the pig in the pond!

And that was the story of Neligan's pig.